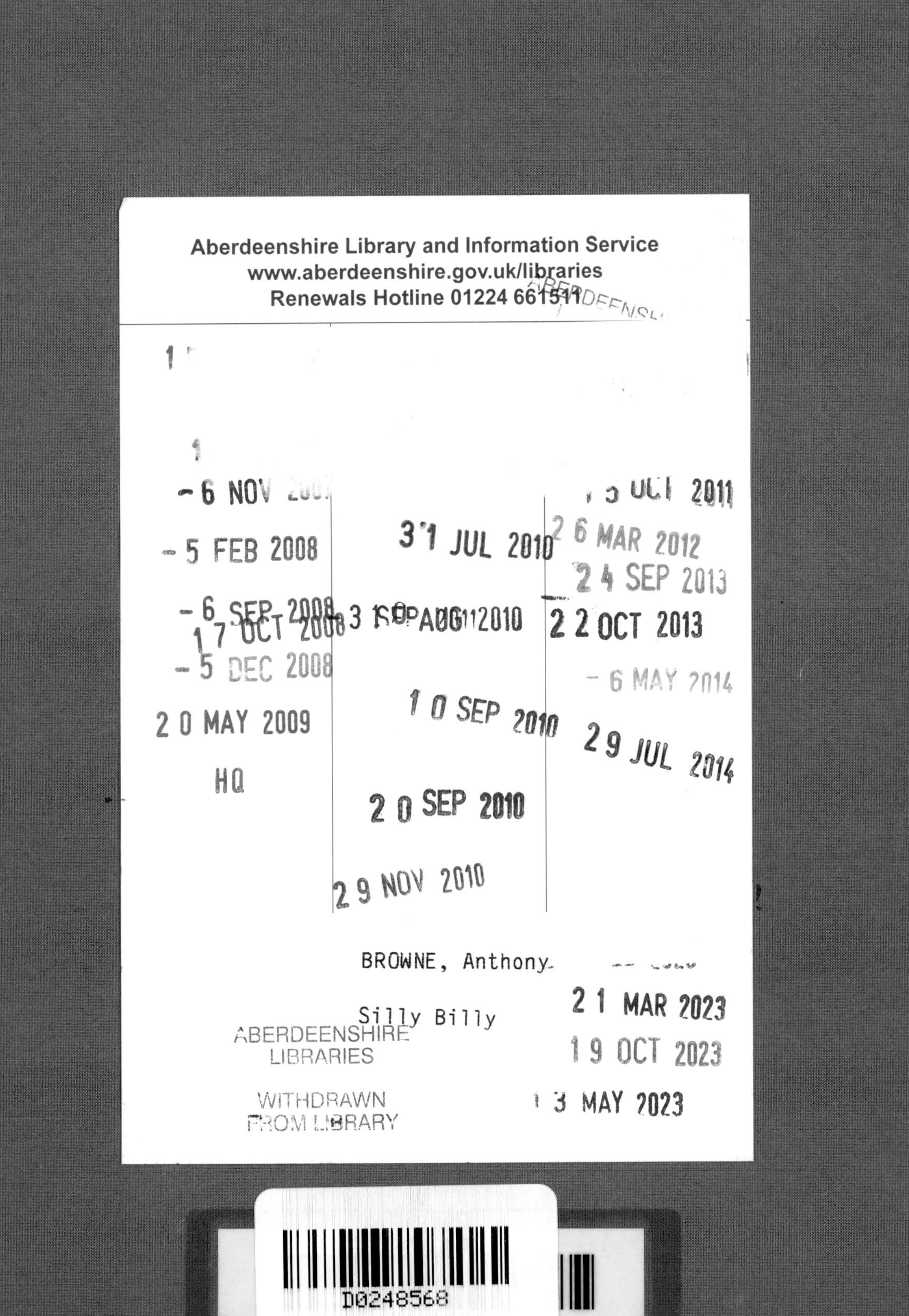

First published 2006 by Walker Books Ltd, 87 Vauxhall Walk, London SE11 5HJ

2 4 6 8 10 9 7 5 3 1

This book has been typeset in Futura

Printed in China

British Library Cataloguing in Publication Data: a catalogue record for this book is available from the British Library

ISBN-13: 978-0-7445-7017-5
ISBN-10: 0-7445-7017-4

www.walkerbooks.co.uk

SILLY BILLY

Anthony Browne

WALKER BOOKS
AND SUBSIDIARIES
LONDON • BOSTON • SYDNEY • AUCKLAND

Billy used to be
a bit of a worrier.

He
worried
about
many things...

Billy worried about **hats**,

and he worried about **shoes**.

Billy worried about **clouds**,

and **rain**.

Billy even worried about **giant birds**.

His dad tried to help.
"Don't worry, lad," he said.
"None of those things could happen.
It's just your imagination."

His mum tried too.
"Don't worry, love," she said.
"We won't let anything
hurt you."

But still Billy worried.

One night he had to
stay with his grandma.
But Billy couldn't sleep.
He was too worried.
He always worried
about staying at other
people's houses.
Billy felt a bit silly,
but at last he got up
and went to tell
his grandma.

"Well fancy that, love," she said. "You're not silly. When I was your age I used to worry like that. I've got just the thing for you."

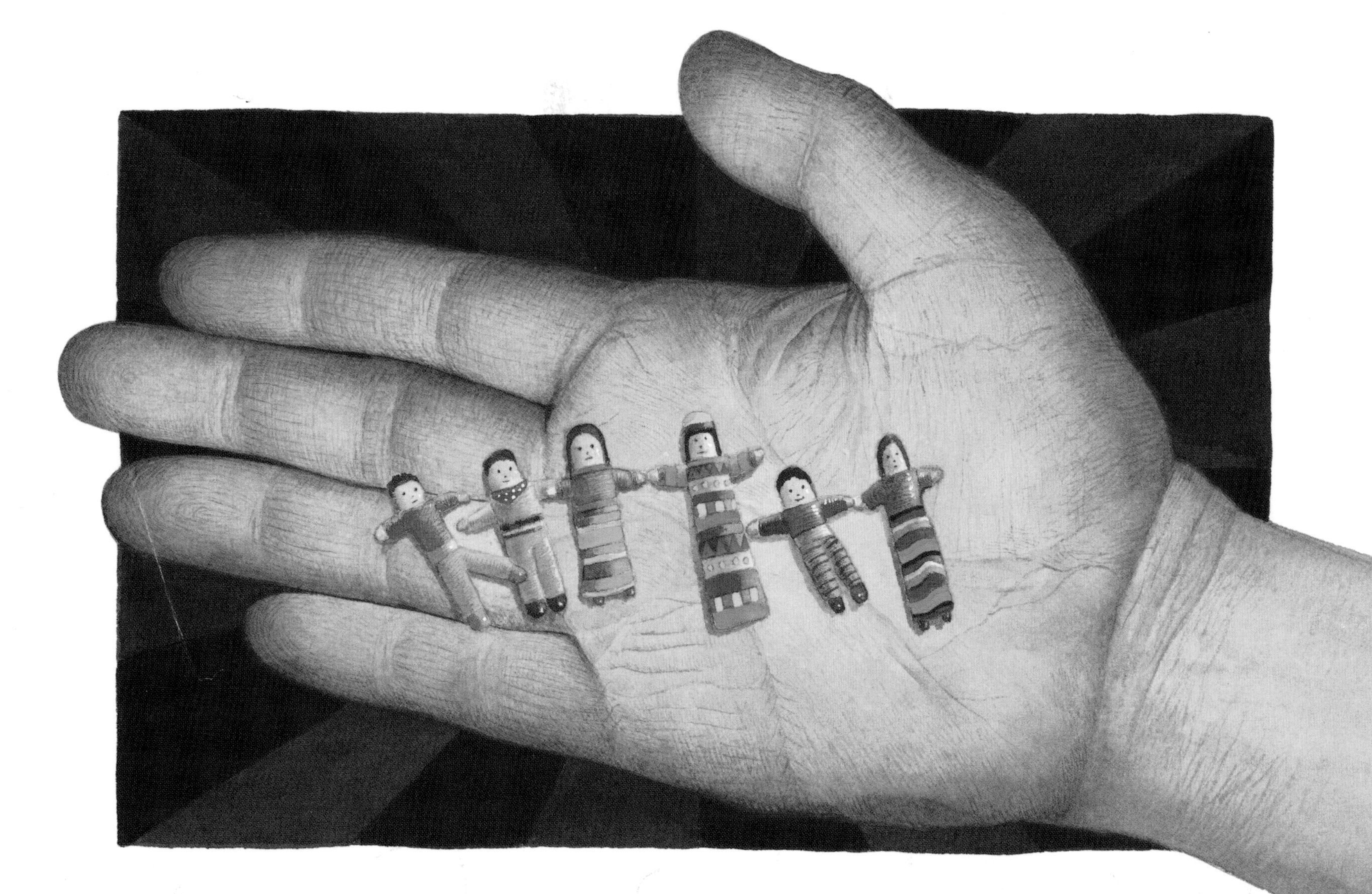

She went into her room and came
out holding something.
"These are worry dolls," she explained.
"Just tell each of them one of your worries
and put them under your pillow. They'll do
all the worrying for you while you sleep."

Billy told all his worries
to the worry dolls.
He slept like a log.

The next morning Billy went home.
That night he again told all his worries
to the dolls. He slept like a stone.

The next night Billy slept well,
and the night after that.

But the night after that Billy started to **worry**.

He couldn't stop thinking about the dolls –
all those **worries** he'd given them...
They must be so worried. It didn't seem fair.

The next day Billy had an idea. He spent all day working at the kitchen table. It was difficult work and at first he made lots of mistakes and had to start again many times.

But finally Billy produced something very special ...

some worry dolls for the worry dolls!

That night EVERYONE slept well.
Billy – and all the worry dolls.

And, after that,
Billy didn't
worry very
much at
all.

And neither did
his friends...
Billy made worry dolls
for ALL of them.

Worry dolls come from the Central American country of Guatemala. They are made from tiny pieces of wood and scraps of cloth and thread. Long ago, the children of Guatemala made these dolls, and when they went to bed at night, they would tell a worry to each one before placing them under their pillows and going to sleep. In this way, they would wake up in the morning feeling much less troubled.

To this day, children in Guatemala trust their dolls to take away their worries as they sleep, and this custom has now spread around the world.